VALENTINE'S DAY

BY GAIL GIBBONS

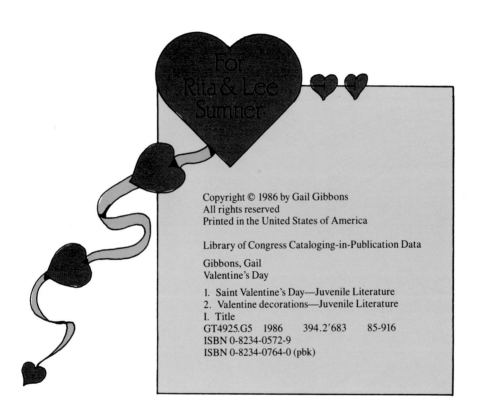

For
Rita & Lee
Sumner

Copyright © 1986 by Gail Gibbons
All rights reserved
Printed in the United States of America

Library of Congress Cataloging-in-Publication Data

Gibbons, Gail
Valentine's Day

1. Saint Valentine's Day—Juvenile Literature
2. Valentine decorations—Juvenile Literature
I. Title
GT4925.G5   1986   394.2′683   85-916
ISBN 0-8234-0572-9
ISBN 0-8234-0764-0 (pbk)

February 14th

Valentine's Day is a special day for love and friendship.
It is celebrated on February 14th.

Many years ago people believed there lived a kind man named Saint Valentine. Valentine's Day is named after him. He was the patron saint of lovers and was friends with many children.

Children would give him letters and flowers to show their love. Perhaps that's how the custom of giving valentine cards began.

People also thought that on the same date
birds chose their mates.

Some young people wanted to choose their sweethearts
by picking a name from a jar.

Today different kinds of valentine cards are given.
There are sweet and loving valentines . . .

and silly ones, too.

There are very fancy valentines,
and others pop up when they are opened.

Some valentines are made at home . . .

and others are bought at stores.

People have always believed that love comes from the heart.

A sweetheart is called a valentine, too.

Some admirers give their valentines flowers on
Valentine's Day . . .

and others give boxes of candy in the shape of a heart.

There are cakes and candies in the shape of a heart, too.
Some even have messages printed on them.

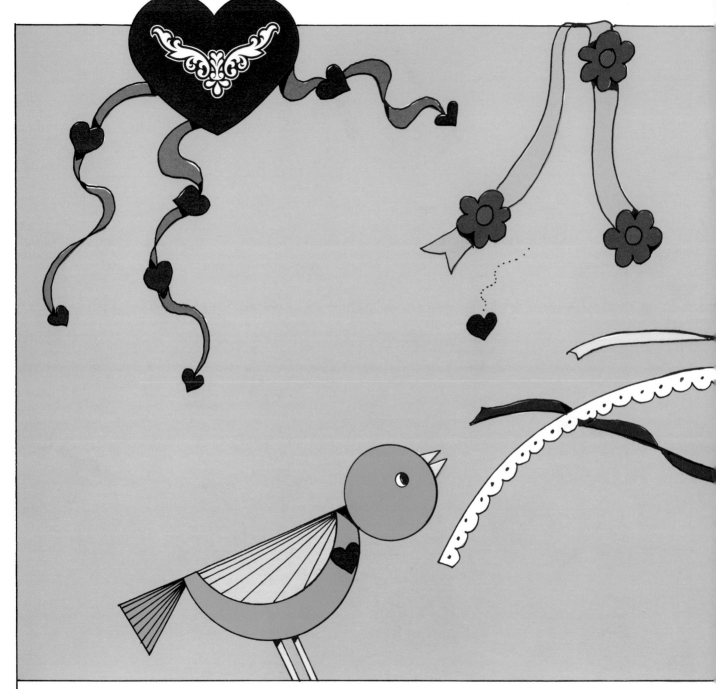

Many decorations are used on Valentine's Day.

There are hearts, laces, ribbons, and flowers . . .

and there is Cupid, too. A long time ago people believed
that when Cupid shot his arrows into their hearts,
they fell in love.

Also, parties are given on Valentine's Day.

Valentine party games are played . . .

and there are lots of goodies to eat.

At other parties, people get their valentines by
bringing special boxes.

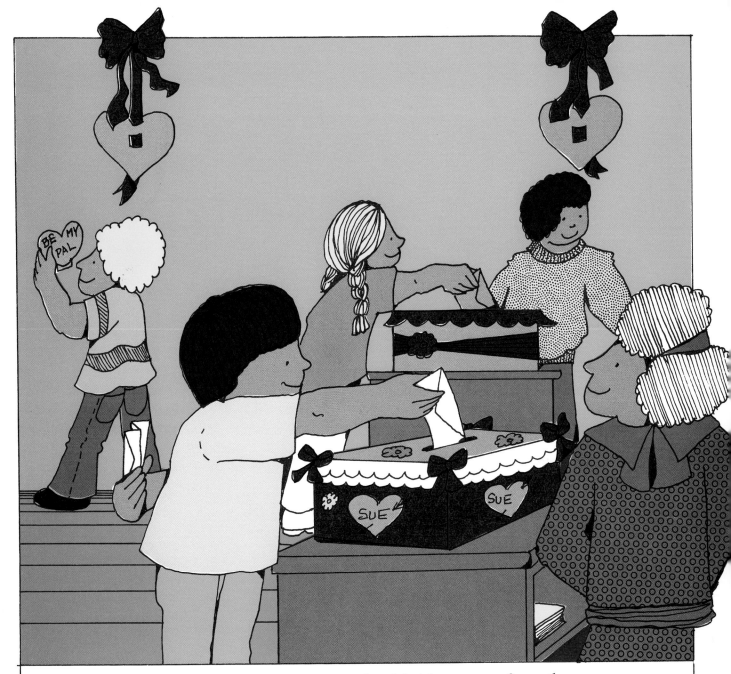

Cards are put in them. Maybe this idea comes from the
time when the names of sweethearts were placed in jars.

Some valentine cards are sent . . .

and happily received.

Valentine's Day is the day for saying "I love you!"

HOW TO MAKE YOUR OWN VALENTINES

YOU NEED: white, pink, and red paper
scissors
glue
lace
stickers
ribbon
crayons

HOW TO DO IT:

STEP 1

Fold one white paper, one pink paper, and one red paper in half.

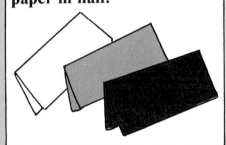

STEP 2

Cut half of a heart shape, like this. Make the white one the biggest, the pink one smaller, and the red one the smallest.

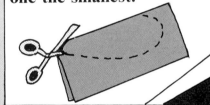

STEP 3

Glue them on top of one another, like this.

STEP 4

Decorate the edges with lace, stickers, and ribbons.

STEP 5

Write a valentine message in the middle.

STEP 6

Have fun making lots of them.

HOW TO MAKE YOUR OWN VALENTINE BOX

YOU NEED: one box
white, pink, and red paper
scissors
glue
lace
stickers
ribbon
crayons

HOW TO DO IT:

♥ STEP 1

Glue the colored paper to the sides of the box, and around the edge and top.

♥ STEP 2

Cut a slot in the top of the box that is big enough for valentines to slip through.

♥ STEP 3

Decorate the box with lace, stickers, and ribbons.

♥ STEP 4

Write your name on the top of the box.

♥ STEP 5

Now you are ready to receive lots of valentines.